THE LOST FRIEND

RUDRAKSH MISHRA

Copyright © Rudraksh Mishra
All Rights Reserved.

Contents

Acknowledgements

ABOUT THE AUTHOR

• v •

Rudraksh Mishra:

Rudraksh Mishra, a young talented author. He describes himself as an authorprenuer, a writing lover from a very young age. As per him he is basically a fictional writer. Got featured in various Magazines. Wrote poems, essays in his childhood. His articles got published in local newspapers too, that was his eureka moment. Became internationally published at the age of just 13.

CONNECT WITH AUTHOR

INSTAGRAM- @author_rudraksh

RU

Prologue

The story removes around life of James the narrator, Drake and Georgina. How they met fell in love, struggled, suffered and supported each other. Drake who became a billionaire was just possible because of support of Georgina and James. Their life went like a roller coaster so many ups and down. The struggles Georgina and James did for Drake in every aspect of his life. Drake a boy who dreamt for a lavish life, faced criticism fought for his dreams.

James:

The best friend of Drake. Drake's childhood friend, His go to person for everything. Went to school with Drake from the start, stood beside Drake on every step of Drake's life.

Georgina:

Childhood friend of Drake. Played a big role in Drake's success.

THE NEVER ENDING BOND

The promise I made to Drake that I will look after his family and Georgina and most importantly never let Georgina be lonely and sad. I was not able to make to the promise I made,Georgina never tried to interact with anyone except her mom, me. She was so broken, missed Drake every second of the day, every thing reminds her of him.

Seeing her downcast and orrowful made me sad too, despite knowing where he went but I couldn't tell her. Although I was aware that if any-day she came to know that all the time I knew where he was , she gonna kill me! but I was bound by a promise that I couldn't break. While lying on my bed many times I thought of breaking the promise and tell her. It was very harsh of me on seeing her grace her joy was all gone, but I was help. It has been 6 years since she didn't attended any party , never socialised not even interested in talking with anyone except a few, faking smile in-front of everyone but almost every night she slept crying remembering him. After his mysterious disappearance, I was seeing him in her, smiling in reply of everyone's comment, hiding her emotions like an emotionless girl, who didn't get hurt no matter what anyone said. Drake was like this he never paid attention to the criticism, hate, opprobrium and so on , he was a clear in his mind from his childhood . I knew Drake from a very long time, we became friends when we were like two years old and in a few years we became best friends. He used to share each and every thing with me, therefore I knew him the most. Being so close for so many years it is very heartbreaking but it is a fact that now we will never be able to live that life again. From last 6 years I have been looking after his family it's my responsibility, they are not only his family members they are mine too.

Since Drake disappeared , Georgina did everything to find him but did not succeed. In the failure of Georgina of not being able to find him, I played a big role as every-time she was close or was about to get a clue I mislead her. After every time she failed she was broken into thousand pieces. Seeing her like that gave me pain too. I comforted her everytime but she only had one task at that time to find Drake. Since I knew where was Drake and if Georgina found out this week secret then our friendship would at be stake and I was pretty sure that this is going to happen someday. Now let me take you deep into our lives.

Drake was born on 6th December in 1973. Drake and I were friends since we were like 2 years old because we were in the same crèche. We both were classmates from the very first day of our schooling career. We always sat together , had lunch together , made infinite memories of school life. Everyone knew that if you find one of us anywhere the other must be near. Our best memories were made our way back to home, laughing , cracking jokes and thus making memories. Two kids with no worries, no frustration, no peer pressure, just one task that is to just enjoy the life. My house was a bit far from Drake's , so when we were kids we were never able to meet after school because I was not able to travel to his house by my own. Drake was an introvert boy, he never liked to interact with anyone never shared his feelings not even with his very close ones. He never liked to talk about people's personal lives, not remembered how many times he debated with the elders on topics like this. They used to say that you are going out of the league so he argued that it is ok to go to out of the league. Actually he was having a far vision which we did not understand, we were just normal kids leading a normal life. I still remember whenever he used to get frustrated he called me and would say, James!! (In an angry voice) and narrated me the entire incident. I talked him out and consoled him, then we cracked some jokes as two best-friends do, you can understand (smiling).

In 1981 , a girl took admission in our school in 3rd Standard. She was admitted in our section. That day *in the 3rd period our class teacher Miss. Britney introduced her to us. Her name was Georgina Phillips, she seemed to be a shy girl , introvert type girl. Later I realised I was wrong, no!! not at all she was very bold , straight forward but yet very helping no matter if you were her friend or not, if you asked her for help she definitely did. She helped Drake a couple of times , help whatever a third class student would need.*

Drake and Georgina talked a little that too only a few times until one day Drake saw Georgina sitting outside her house , Drake went inside his house and told his mom about Georgina, His mom called Georgina's mom and comforted her that she is keeping Georgina till she come back so she don't need not to worry. His mom Mrs. Bereth went to Georgina and asked her to come to her house till her mom come back , Georgina accepted this happily as Drake's and Georgina's parents became good friends and good neighbours too. Since then Georgina and Drake started involving with each other, they made a routine to play in evening whether at Drake's home or Georgina's that doesn't matter. They became open to each other , Drake enjoyed her company more than she enjoyed because , Drake as an introvert like someone who can start the conversation, can understand his emotions and unexpressed feelings and Georgina had all of them. After this they both started talking in school also , they became friends eventually good friends. Georgina became my friend too, the road on which me and Drake used to travel holding hands , laughing and giggling now Georgina also joined us. We were in 5th class at that time, I remember we three walking beside our cycles and we three talking and laughing unnecessarily, it was then but then it was true. We all three were good friends but no one noticed when we became best friends. Sharing each and every thing we three developed a never-ending bond. Made a fixed time to meet and enjoy, and I or even none of us noticed that we were addicted to each other if we don't meet, our day was like incomplete. That's how our relation transformed from being a new student or a stranger to a known class-fellow, from being a class-fellow to a good Friend and best-friends. Drake and Georgina spent more time together as they were neighbours and I was about one and a half kilometre away. The interesting thing is that from a group of 2 it became a group of 3 idiots and from 3 it became a group of 4. How come 4?? Is this a question that arose in your mind. Eva Williams was the 4th one. A creative girl, sort of very techy. She and Drake used to plan for Drake's business strategies and all.

Eva Williams, when Georgina was admitted to our section then in 3rd class Eva became her good friend and from 3rd class to 7th class and still counting they are best friends. So both of us got a company. From 7th we 4 stayed together until Drake went and broke our group. You know that Drake and Georgina's house was 1 and a half kilometres far from my house, yes but the fun fact is that I hesitated cycling that one and a half kilometre but I cycled 3 kilometres many times to Eva's house, actually she was far away from us so

Georgina and Drake couldn't cycle and go there every other day but I have to because I didn't wanted that she would feel that she is outcasted. Georgina and Eva were almost same in nature and Drake and me were almost same so indirectly we all 4 were somehow similar to each other. Days passed our bond grew even more stronger. Each of us was almost clear what they have do in life, Drake was the odd one out, his dreams was out of our thinking capacity. The amount hard work he did at that age was the reason he got early success that too big success. In 9th standard all 4 of us decided to arrange a party at Drake's house, we played games, had a fun chat and many more. That party was not just a casual party.(you will read more about this party in next chapter)

MAKING THE BILLIONAIRE

Drake's dream was to be a billionaire. From a very young age he made it clear in his mind that he is going to be a billionaire and live his dream life. He was in 7th standard he asked me that he had wanted to join a 4 month course of Website development , we were just around 12 or 13 and he was looking very clear towards his future. I didn't had any idea what was all that back then so I was listening to him without any spells on my tongue but I gave my full support, but I did not demotivated him. Tried my best I did whatever I could. Those period of about 7-8 years was very tough for him, he fought with himself everyday at night, he asked him many times that will I be able to do it? , but his answer was always yes. He faced tons of comments on his behaviour, he fought with criticism with giving criticisers a smile. He was very self confident sometimes people used to call him arrogant but actually if he was not like that he would never be able to do what he did. Georgina was one of the biggest or you can say the biggest supporter of Drake, she did everything that Drake asked.

The course which Drake wanted to take in 7th standard was all possible because of Georgina, Drake told me one evening that he wanted to take that course so he asked me to talk to his mom. I was hesitating to talk to his mom and convince her. Georgina was noticing from 4-5 days that Drake seemed to be sad and tensed, Drake was ignoring Georgina for about a week and then Georgina asked me, I hesitated at first and avoided telling her but she kept on asking so I told her that Drake want to join a course but he want me to convince her mom and I am not sure how to start the conversation. I told her a little about Drake's dream, what was he willing to do. She seemed like she did not understood about his dream, the way she reacted it was clear that she thought that his dream was unreal and boring. She did not replied at that time she just said bye to me and left. I thought she developed a feeling that Drake is boring I mean just a day dreamer and like that. My biggest fear at that juncture was if by chance started to ignore Drake or not behaved the way she was behaving then Drake would have killed me.

I went to bed and started planning how to talk to Drake's mom and help Drake. That night I slept at 4 AM, in the morning I decided to go to Drake's home and try to convince her mom but I was not able to go to his house. Unfortunately I went out of town with mom for about a week, when I came back, I went to Drake's house to apologise and convince his mom for allowing him to take the course but when I went to his house, I went upstairs straight to his room, he was there reading a book I saw the name " THE MONEY MIND " the book name was. I was shocked how he purchased that book, I asked him" Hey Bug (Drake's nickname by which me and Georgina used to called him).

how did your mum agreed to buy you this book and what about the course. He did not replied , he ignored me. Hey! Bug! Drake! what happened tell me, he ignored me again. I sat on a chair and was irritated. There was an awkward silence in the room for about 5 minutes. Drake! are you sure you don't want to talk to me? I thought he would say sorry or something like that but he said that " James can go out of my room" I was in shock and I went out of his room I closed the door angrily and went downstairs. Her mom was making food I went to kitchen asked aunt if there was something to eat. She gave me cookies and made me a cup of coffee. We started chatting with each other. We had a chat like normal, she asked about my mom and all. After I finished eating I was about to leave, I was in the veranda and was going to my cycle and then I saw Georgina coming. She saw me and waved at me "what's up dude?" She asked, I was not in a situation to talk. She stopped and recalled my name " hey jammy, hey! " So many things were going in my mind that I was not able to reply correctly but whatever I just told her everything that took place with me in Drake's house about 20 minutes ago. I cannot understand anything Jammy. I asked her to stop for a couple of minutes. I wanted to ask her if she knew what happened with Drake why was he behaving like that, and how did he got the book. Our conversation was :

Me: Hey! GD (nickname by which only I used to call her, it was a secret name made by herself) do you know what happened to Drake and how did aunt agreed to buy the book?

Georgina: Do you mean that money book I mean the book about earning money I think, that one?

Me: Yes! That one.

Georgina: Oh! Her mom agreed.

Me: Ok that is good but how?

Georgina: Actually that day when you told me about that course and all, I went to back to home and straight to bed and started thinking about him. I did a research about that course for my knowledge. The other day when I went to Drake's house, I talked to his mom I mean not directly but yes, I did talked to her. I had a long chat with his mom about that course and she decided and that book was a gift from me.

Me: Oh! Thank you, as you know that he asked me earlier to help him but unfortunately I was not able to. So you did a great help to me. Well I am having no clue why Drake is not talking to me, not sure what is in his mind right now.

Georgina: Not talking to you? He missed you all these 6-7 days. When I gave him the book, despite the happiness of the Book, the first thing he said was that where is James?

Me: Oh! then why is not talking to me

Georgina: No idea, you know he is Drake. Well you come with me.

I went to his room accompanied by Georgina, He saw and was replying to her but was ignoring me. Georgina asked him why is he ignoring me, is there something wrong that James did. He did not replied but Georgina kept asking, after about 2 minutes he took a deep breath and said " no James never did anything" I knew that there was something fishy going on in his mind. I again said hello to Drake this time he replied "hi jammy" now Georgina looked to me and said see I told you. Apparently we (Georgina and me) both were right as Drake was not replying me before and Georgina said to me that Drake was not angry with me. We all three stayed there for about half an hour, talked and enjoyed. We three the trio from which almost every neighbourhood lady was fed up!. We broke window and flower pots of almost every house in the colony. Drake never played with any other boy of his colony in short in his neighbourhood only Georgina was his friend in fact his best friend though. So when we three used to play or you can say we two as Drake was made referee most of time whenever me and Georgina played a match. He did not like to play football, he is a great watched of football but he never completed a single match which he played. So whenever any lady came to complain his mom or if the one who is the sufferer from our ball starts shouting or scolding Drake or me Georgina always replied them back and stood by our side. I remember once we were playing football and I broke a decorative item of one of my neighbour and that house was of the strictest lady in Drake's colony, so she (the house owner) came out in a hurried way I knew she was angry and would erupt in a few moments. Me and Drake were ready to run but Georgina went close to her and asked for the ball. The lady picked up the ball and said that she will never give the ball and started shouting that you all are mad peoples I will tell to your mom and all. Me and Bug both knew that Georgina was going to erupt and within few seconds Georgina replied "don't your kids play, your Daughter broke my keychain and damn whole canvas. I never complained, and Drake and Jammy never hit the ball a single time today then why are you shouting their name" The lady got angry too and she slapped Georgina, now our very unique Georgina after getting slapped, she said "now can I take my ball aunt" and that was quite like a humiliation for that lady but Georgina is one of it's kind. We all loved each others company very much, we all could understand each, cared for each other's emotions but never showed off. We made so much memories together, those days were unforgettable.

Drake started being busy with his works and after everything he had to do school work also. He was not avoiding or ignoring us, it was so hectic for him that he was not able to play or having another fun with us. Georgina was his neighbour so she was able to meet him twice or thrice but I was around 2 kilometres far from their house so I was not able and of course we were in 10ᵗʰ class so our schedule was hectic. Drake's attendance started decreasing as he wanted time. He was doing good, only I knew what was his plan for the next 2-3 years. He was all clear in his mind, what when and the most important how, the answer was with him and that is the most important.

In the journey of Drake becoming a billionaire I did supported him but but but, the major support was from Georgina. She stood by him in everything, she faced criticism with Drake, whosoever said anything to Drake and all the negative things and comments that he faced and never got affected that all was possible because of Georgina. Drake broke many times he lost hope many times that he will never be able to do what he wished but Georgina motivated him. She did her homework, school assignments so that he can concentrate on his projects. She stayed at his house completed his school notebooks and many things in-short she was like a pillar for him.

Drake was in 10th when he decided to start the journey of becoming a entrepreneur. I remember that Drake told me about his plan, I was spellbound. I asked him that did he told GD about the plan, I was sure that how can Drake not tell this to GD, but to my surprise Bug did not told to GD, he felt shy in telling her, I started laughing, just think that he was feeling shy from a girl who was his best Friend from 5th class. I mocked him a little about him and Georgina. Do you know what he did to me when I mocked something about GD, Bug slapped me, I mean not seriously but In a friendly way and he said that "she is my best friend and best friend nothing else and I feel shy telling her because I need some amount of money to start and if I will tell her then she will start trying to arrange the money " that is what he said, he was not wrong I later realised. After that we started discussing about what to do, how to accomplish and the most important how to start. To do all of those, he was in need of money. Now again he asked me to help him. I was not sure how could I have helped him. He was in need of money and I was not able to help him so I was very guilty, every time I saw him tensed, sad. He did not told his mom about his plan. He was in need of about 3 or 4 hundred dollars. You can understand how touch was it to arrange four hundred dollars for a 14-15 years old boy.

It has been 2 weeks now and still we were not able to arrange the money. We were still thinking how to arrange the money. We were struggling did everything what we could, but we were not unsuccessful. Drake was sad and he was kind of confused what to do now. I was helpless but I had an idea. I went to Georgina's house without telling Drake. I knocked at the door many times but there was no response, I rang the bell 2-3 times but again no responce, I waited 10 minutes, but no response was coming from inside. I was thinking what to do and I was with no clue so I decided to go back, I was about to leave in between that Georgina opened the door, and called my name " Jammy! where are you going? I looked back and saw her so I again moved close to her and we waved at each other. She asked me to come inside her house, I was feeling awkward but I went inside her house. We started talking. We were hungry by now and GD brought white sauce pasta which she made by herself for me and Drake. After some chatting, I was making myself ready to tell her about Bug's future plan and that he was in need of money but GD interrupted me and said that Bug has not talked to her from last 2 weeks, he was avoiding to be in contact with her. After some time I started to talk about problem which me and Bug were in. I told her everything, I was in flow and I kept saying continuously for 10 minutes without giving her a chance to say something. After she listened what I told, she said " why Bug do not trust me, I told him so many times that he should tell me everything but he never tell me." She asked me to wait and went to Drake's house, this put me in tension and I went behind Georgina and she banged the door, shouted his name. I tried to stop her but she was furious, she did not listened to me at all. Drake came opened door, he was about to open his mouth but Georgina slapped him not once she smacked his face. He was in shock his mouth was wide open, his eyes were moving right to left, left to right seeing Georgina's face. Georgina pushed him inside the house and shut the door. I was thinking whether to go inside the house or not. I was thinking about Drake, what was Georgina must be doing. After few minutes I moved towards his house and knocked the door, was nervous but knocked harder, GD opened the door. I went inside Drake was sitting on couch. He rushed on me when he saw me asked me why did I told her. She came and said "Bug! Were you stupid from birth or you did a course for becoming so stupid." That roast made me laugh hard, she roasted him. Bug was again spell-bounded, the roast king was silent and smiling. He asked Georgina why he is a stupid in a sarcastic way. Georgina was not in a mood to hear a joke she slapped him again. I was shocked and was a bit terrified. I held GD in my hands and took her in a different room. She was angry at me and said "Jammy what are you doing? I want to talk to Drake. Leave me" I tried to make her calm and tried to have a chat with her but she was in a different world. I gave her a glass of water and then asked her that she should talk with Drake but first be calm. She listened to me and took a deep breath and waited for 2-3 minutes and then she got up and opened the door, she went close to Bug and made him sit down and sat beside him too. I too went there and sat on a chair.

Georgina, looked at me with a innocent baby face, her chin trembling, wet eyes. She hugged both of us and started crying. I slowly moved myself and went out of the house so that they can handle themselves. I was literally very confused where to go now, back home or stay at GD's house. I knew that she would come back to talk with me. I was in her drawing room seeing the decoration of the room. 30 minutes passed away GD still in his house! I decided to go back so I was moving to exit but GD came back and asked me "oh! Jammy you are still here? I mean I thought you would have gone back. Yeah! I am about to leave so excuse me and I am going I said and I was little bit angry at that time. She stopped me and said "hey! Jammy wait dude! Where are you going. I want to talk with you I have a plan." Plan what plan and plan for what, I asked her. Dude plan for Drake's career man! She exclaimed. Oh yeah, got it I said. Then we started discussing and kept discussing for about 20 minutes. Her idea was great but it was literally very tough to execute. We were discussing and the door bell rang, she opened the door and it was her mom. She came inside and saw me "oh James you are also here oh good. So guys what's going on" nothing just chilling and having fun Georgina replied. Oh good go on her mom said. Our planning was done so I said bye to her and it was decided that we will start our plan next week. It was 6 'o' clock by then. I went back home. Days passed, the day came our plan was to be started this day. As per our plan I informed my mother that I have to go out for an important work or a part time work you can say. So I moved, according to the plan I had to do part time jobs as many as 2-3 so with that I could arrange around 100 dollars and me and Georgina combined had 100 dollars, Georgina said that she will ask her mother for 100 dollars no matter how but she will manage and the rest 100 dollars was the only problem we were stuck. So as per plan I was in out of my home town, now I was looking for jobs. For completing the task I had to do 2-3 jobs per day, that means I had to go for short timed jobs. It took me almost 2 days to get a job that fits perfectly on our plan. I did not slept a single minute two days straight. I got 2 jobs, I gave tuitions to 4-5 children those were in 4th standard students, and one was in 7th standard. Second job was working in shops, took care of shop worked as salesman. I did those for about a month and It was a very unique experience for me but I earned about 97 dollars. I came back home back to my town, oh! What an feeling was that. It was night when I came back, I waited for next day, I was not able to sleep that night. In the morning as the sun rose up, I rode to her house, was so excited that I was singing the whole way to her house, people were staring at me but I was in my own mad world. As soon as I reached her house I smacked the door of her house and I was continuously knocking. I heard someone coming closer, Georgina opened the door and said "what!! Are you mad Jammy? I heard you knocked the door why are you just knocking like a psycho" I started laughing and she was getting annoyed by this, as usual she slapped me I became silent immediately. Then asked her to come inside and we moved to her room, I sat on her bed and then I asked her that how much money she was able to arrange. She gave a wicked smile and said "Jammy! I am not able to collect much money" I said that it is ok, I was trying to comfort her that we will manage but then she started laughing and said " dude chill man! I got 190 dollars with me" I was surprised, how did she managed this much. I asked her but she was not answering. After 2-3 minutes of pin drop silence she broke the silence and said dude I sold my watch and you know I contacted students and offered them a help that I will complete their homework in return of money and I did not slept a hour from last 4 days. Now I was just shocked and was laughing, I was happy we were happy, we did it, we shouted. What about the 100 dollars which your mom has to give? I asked. She gave it dude she replied. So basically we did it and we were excited to tell this to Bug. We decided to go to his house in noon and surprise him. In between that we ate snacks and my favourite lemonade, I mean lemonade which Georgina makes. So I drank lemonade, had fun and then we decided to go to Drake's house. We moved outside of the house and then moved towards Drake's house. We knocked the door. He opened the door and I was about to say but Georgina jumped on him, she hung on him crossed her legs around her waist and literally they were looking cute together. I too went to him and gave him a tight hug, he was in surprise that why we were hugging and joyful. We made him sat down on the couch and made him relaxed. After 5-10 minutes, I closed his eyes and GD took 419 dollars out from her purse and handed them to Drake. He immediately pushed me and saw that what he felt was right, those were 419 dollars in his hand. The first question he asked was "how you both arranged" we both tried our best to change the topic but he was stuck on only one thing that how we arranged. So after all we had to surrender in front of him and tell him. I narrated him the whole planning and execution. I told her every thing except that Georgina sold her watches because GD warned me earlier that if I tried to tell him she will kill me. After listening everything Drake had his eyes wet he hugged me, he kept talking to me and thanking and all that only with me for about 10 minutes. I saw Georgina she was not jealous or something like that but she sold her watches for him and most of all she liked him. She was having tears in her eyes so I whispered Drake to thank Georgina. Drake now realised that she was also there, he turned and thanked Georgina but GD was about to hug him but he moved away, he was not able to see that GD was hugging him. That was sad for Georgina.

The journey for Drake becoming a billionaire had begun. That was the first step. Nobody was having any sort of idea that the boy who was an average student and an introvert will be the youngest billionaire in the world. He was 15 when we arranged 400 dollars for his startup idea and in 1991 he became a millionaire, then he was 18.

IN NEXT CHAPTER YOU WILL GO THROUGH THE LAVISH LIFE HE LIVED.

CHAPTER THREE

THE YOUNG GUN

Drake, an ordinary boy who became a sensation, idol of many entrepreneurs. The youngest millionaire and youngest billionaire too. The age where life takes turn and it is the most enjoyable too, so being financially independent at that age is the best feeling and that too a millionaire. His startups were now one of the biggest brand set ups. His clothing brand, his food chains, his webs, tech startup spread all over the world.

The first thing, the first big thing he bought was a villa, it was big enough for our whole colony to live in. The villa consisted a separate portion for me and Georgina. Our name was written on the top front face of particular villa of both of us. He moved there with his parents, after few weeks Georgina too moved there with his family. They asked me many times to shift there but I was hesitating, but they both wished me to be with them, but actually I felt awkward like I am disturbing Georgina's privacy. One night someone knocked at my door, it was 2 of night, my whole family was surprised and everyone thought that those were thieves except me "after a while I screamed and said why will any thief knock and come, let's open the door" after I opened the door I saw GD there, she held my collar and pulled towards her and she then threw me!! And two bodyguards I think they were bodyguards, made me sit in the car, I was furious and was angry at GD. Was not sure what will she do but was sure that she will never do something bad to me, but still very confused. She took me to the villa, she took my family too.

That place was an enormous one, a swimming pool, three separate villas for me, GD and Drake. Drake was fond of cars from a very young age and when he became a millionaire he was living his dream, at that time he was owning 8 cars, his favourite was his Lexus. Interior of his room was filled with expensive items, in short he lived all his life lavishly. He gifted me and Georgina perfumes worth 25,000 dollars. I never used it that is another thing but yeah he never showed off that he was a millionaire or billionaire he always behaved like he used to with us.

Hustle, his clothing brand was one of the biggest brand in terms of brand value. His clothing brand spread all over the world. Hustle's t-shirt were of handsome amount. At first his brand was only for t-shirts but slowly slowly it grew into a biggie multinational brand. He was successful he did it. I did not became a billionaire but I was very happy. He was my brother from birth and he was a billionaire so it was a proud moment for me. We all three were doing good, Drake asked me many times to join him and became his partner but every time I denied. Georgina got even more closer with Drake's family. He was a celebrity, he was not a Hollywood star or a sportsmen but, he was so influencing and he used to spend so lavishly that he grabbed attention of the youth and young entrepreneurs. He became an ideal entrepreneur for most of the teens who wanted to be an entrepreneur. At that time he had 9 mobiles (sell phones), 10 or 20 shoes and each pair of shoes was of about 150 euros, that is still a good amount for shoes and at that time it was like a dream to buy those shoes. He was fond of cars from childhood and now he was able to ride any car he wished. As in 1998 he had 29 cars, 17 bikes, 4 cruise, 4 bungalow and most importantly in 1999 he built a palace named "Drake's Ism" yes Drake's Ism not Drakism. He was self obsessed, his plans which only I and GD knew were darker than the black colour, I mean they were not bad but those ideas, his thinking was leading him to destructive way. He always wanted to be the best, that is a good thing but his thinking was like, he has to win no matter how. Me and Georgina tried many times to make him understand that this was not good for mental health but he always replied the same "History and world only remembers the winner, till you are on the winning side, you are good" I knew he was not saying anything wrong but he cannot be the winner all his life and yes! The habit of being at the top and being the best took his interest in life, no he is not dead, maybe by the time you be reading this, he would be dead but till now, he is alive.

CHAPTER FOUR

THE TURNING POINT

Till year 2000 everything was fine and going good but from the mid-2000 the downfall of Drake and his empire began. Dralicious, his food chain was banned in about 19 countries, including U.S.A, U.S.S.R, Spain, France and 15 more. This gave him a big loss. Stocks of his restaurant fell down like a ball on a down inclined path. His clothing brand Hustle was the biggest brand from 1990-1996, and in 1998 his brand faced a massive decrease in sales as one of the biggest brand of all time Fendy again topped the market and big brands like Allen Solly and Puma were handling the market and this blew Hustle away. Well if Drake would have continued, His brand would be surviving till date, but his mental attitude that he must be a winner, from a very young age he was facing criticism but then nothing happened to him but now when he was a billionaire and his wealth decreased from 56 billion to 24 billion U.S dollars, he was broken into thousand pieces. He sold his palace for 900 million dollars that was not the real price, it would be sold for more but at that time it was emergency. His ships were not doing anything now, his overseas business stopped. His wealth was 56 billion dollars so you can understand how expensive his daily life must be and if someone drops from there it is very tough for him or her to get up and rise but not everyone is like the Phoenix.

In 2002 his wealth fell to 20 million US dollars and he was almost bankrupt I mean not bankrupt but so many loans and shares so he was with no money in comparison with his expenses not the lavishness just the necessity and the loans , he had to manage shares also, and he was thinking to make his brand alive once more but he was not able to as all the big daddy billionaires were against him. So one day he called me and told me that he want to meet me right now, I was scared that he must be thinking of doing something even worse and yes! I was right. When I met him, he hugged me and said that he like Georgina and love him, I knew that. I felt relieved but that was not the matter, after some chatting he surprisingly handed me his will, yes he was ready with a will. I was surprised and I said "are you mad or what Drake?" He said "brother take this and don't tell anyone that I am going and will never come back." Never comeback what I said, my eyes were wet. He replied "jammy, listen dude, do not worry about me, I am going to the path of spirituality, I will never come back to this world, this holy fake world" Wait a minute! Where are you going, am I capable of knowing this, I asked jokingly. "India" he replied. Where in India I asked. somewhere between Shivalik range dude. I was about to ask him some more but hugged me and gave me promise of his life that I should never tell about his existence to anyone.

Since then, I met him only two times and yes! I am looking after his family and Georgina from last 19 years and I will till my last breath. Georgina was broken, her grace, her smile was all gone. GD, this nickname is very simple G= Georgina, D= Drake, but Drake never understood. He was not living a life, he was in a race all his life. His was good in life but he was chasing money and luxury, but that was hurting his mind, the mental attitude he had from start hurried him badly. When he faced the loss, he found himself lost in a mere land, he tried to fight back but the fact was that he lost his interest in the life and was willing to give up, I gave him many lectures but he took those in wrong way and went to India. In Shiwalik ranges there was a chain of hermitage, so he met the head, he was very eager to join that hemitage. He made a will and then one day he left for India. After that I met him once.

Georgina was like a living dead body. As per me Drake was wrong what he did was wrong I mean that was his life but what he did was not an appropriate way to fight any problem, and that too without informing the person who struggled so much just for his dream. I found a poem in Georgina's diary, which she wrote in his memories.

His smile was like grace

Though it cannot be replaced .

His laughter so loud

It echoed through the crowd.

His perfume scent so sweet

Without it I feel incomplete

His presence was warm

Now gone, we are left to mourn.

It was a Friday

He sat on his driveway

Tears ran down his cheeks

Writing a letter he let his heart speak.

Feeling all alone

He felt he world was a cyclone

A beautiful soul

His mind with a hole

He hid her depression

with no expression he hid his sadness

From all this madness

He was hurting

convinced he was a burden

Soon things got bad

His heart was sad.

Destiny, a very beautiful thing. After so many years Georgina was tired, she too decided to give up and go. I tried to stop her but when she told the name of the place she was going I let her go and I decided go with her too for sometime. It was the same place where Drake went. The day came Georgina was on the same land. Unfortunately Drake was out of that land, within these years Drake became a senior man in the town, his head was not present there so he was on a tour to all the places where this hermitage was. I enquired to the locals that when will he be back, they told that he will be back after 1 month. I decided to wait for the auspicious moment when Georgina will meet Drake. Days passed, only 2 days left. Georgina was feeling relaxed but still Drake was in her mind almost every time.

It was the night of the last day of wait. The next day Drake was to be back, I was not able to sleep, so I decided to go outside in fresh air, there I saw Georgina. We had a chat for about half an hour and then she went in her room. Now the day was here, the people were excited, they were preparing for a grand welcome of Drake. Drake was half way to main gate when he heard someone yelling Drake and no one knew that his name was Drake, that was Georgina, she saw him and immediately ran toward him, this time I did not stopped her. She hugged him, she was crying tremendously, everyone was seeing them.

Drake looked at me and asked me why she is here and I just waved my shoulders, we had a chat in just eye contact. After some time Georgina came to me and was exclaiming that see, Drake is here, when I replied that yes I know and I was aware that he was here. She was shocked and started slapping me. The last time we three hugged each other and they both stayed there together. That was the last time I met them..... I am planning to have a visit there. Hope I will be able to meet them....

"THE DESTINED COUPLE"

\\\\\\\\\\\\\\\\\\\\\\\\\\

www.ingramcontent.com/pod-product-compliance
Lightning Source LLC
Chambersburg PA
CBHW031005180726
47993CB00018B/1579